Fantastic Folk Tales

THE HORN THAT COULD HEAR

Russian Folk Tale

An imprint of Om Books International

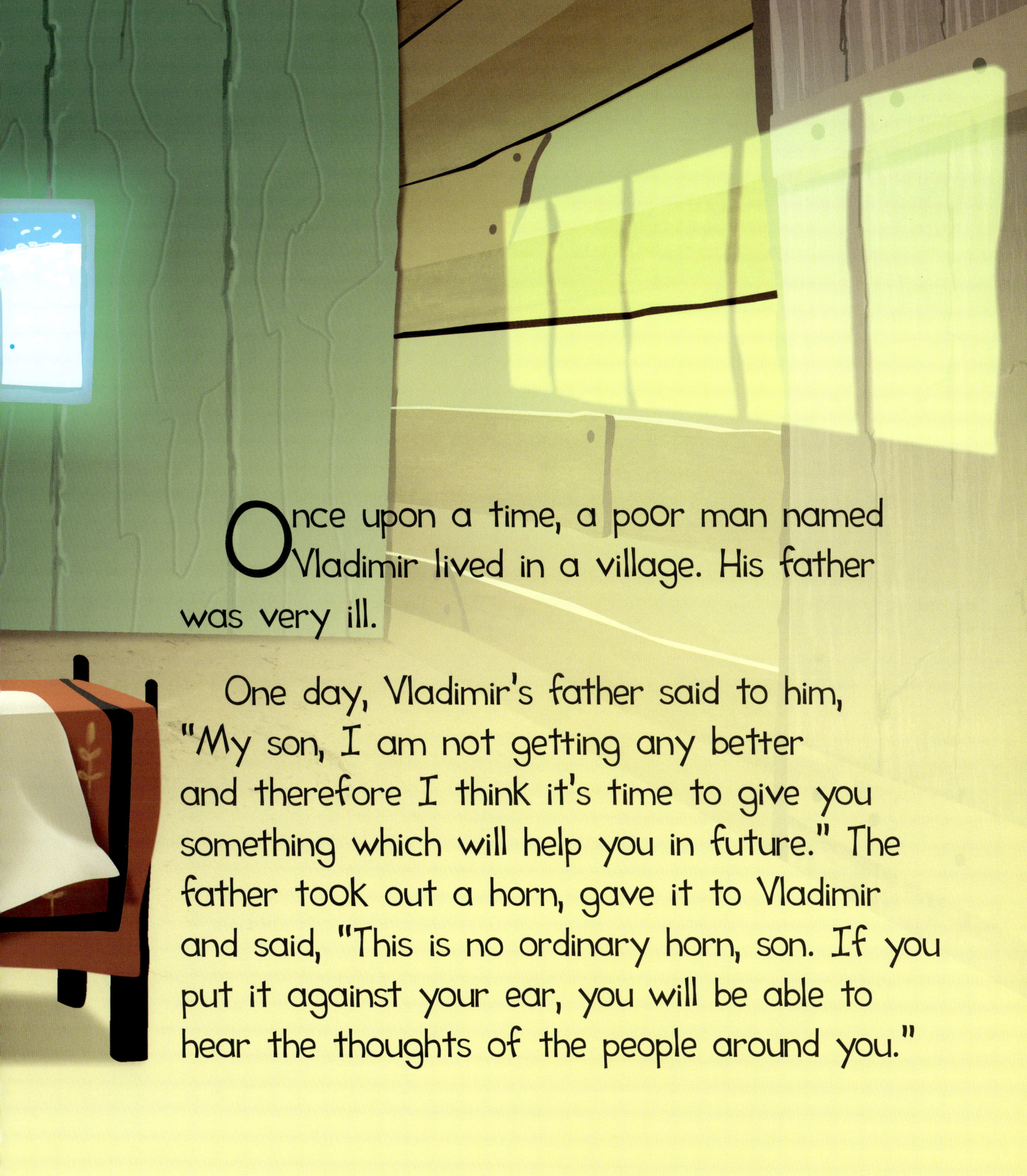

Once upon a time, a poor man named Vladimir lived in a village. His father was very ill.

One day, Vladimir's father said to him, "My son, I am not getting any better and therefore I think it's time to give you something which will help you in future." The father took out a horn, gave it to Vladimir and said, "This is no ordinary horn, son. If you put it against your ear, you will be able to hear the thoughts of the people around you."

After his father died, Vladimir decided to travel and look for a job somewhere. After many days, he came to a stone castle on the road. Vladimir went inside and met with the owner of the castle, a long-haired giant.

With a quivering voice, Vladimir said, "Greetings, Sir! My name is Vladimir and I am travelling from place to place looking for some work. I would be very grateful if you could employ me as your cook."

The giant agreed to the proposal. As Vladimir went towards the kitchen and away from the giant, he took out his horn to hear the giant's thoughts. He heard the giant thinking, *Let's see if this man proves to be a good cook. Otherwise, I'll just eat him up!*

Vladimir froze. He realised that he was trapped in the castle and would have to prove to be a good cook till he could plan his escape! He cooked the best dish for the giant. The giant was really impressed with the food and allowed Vladimir to stay. Vladimir continued cooking the giant's meals while looking for an escape passage in the huge castle.

One day, when Vladimir went to the basement which was dark and gloomy, he heard someone crying. He spotted a beautiful girl tied to a pillar, crying. He asked her, "Who are you and why are you here?" The girl replied, "I am the princess of this kingdom and this castle belongs to me. The giant killed my father, the king, took over the castle and the kingdom and made me a prisoner." Vladimir was shocked and said, "Don't worry, I will rescue you!" The princess asked, "How will you rescue me? You will never be able to escape this castle unless the giant dies. And he is very strong!" Vladimir realised that the princess was right but he refused to give up.

Shortly afterwards, Vladimir went to the room where the giant was sitting and took out his horn. He heard the giant's thought, *Where is the cook? I hope he never finds out about the princess. Even if he does, he will not be able to escape before I die. Who will ever tell him that the secret to my strength is my long hair?*

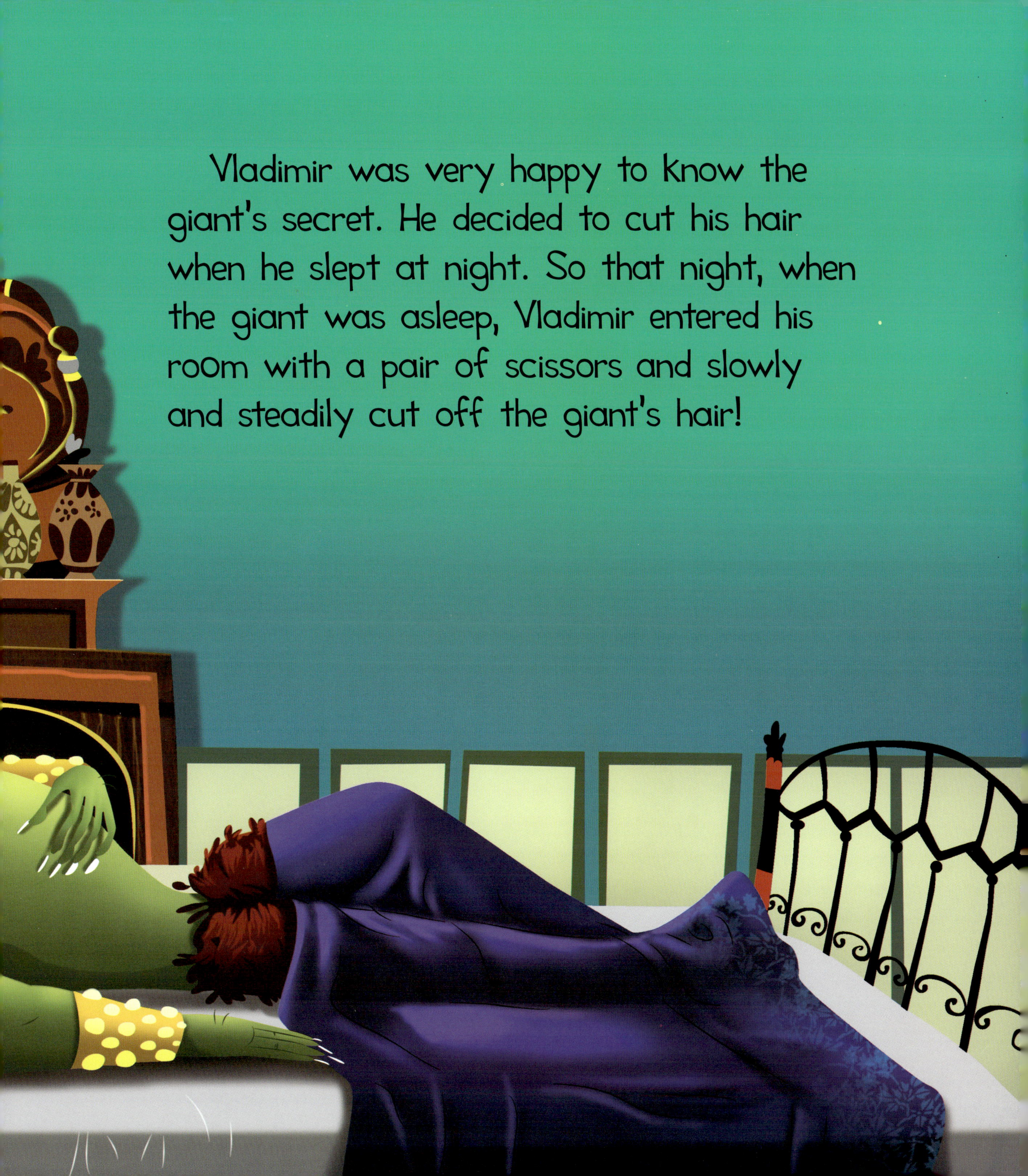

Vladimir was very happy to know the giant's secret. He decided to cut his hair when he slept at night. So that night, when the giant was asleep, Vladimir entered his room with a pair of scissors and slowly and steadily cut off the giant's hair!

When the giant woke up the next morning feeling very weak, he realised that someone had cut his hair. Now anybody could defeat or even kill him! He ran away from the castle, as fast as his legs could carry him!

Vladimir freed the princess. They fell in love and soon married each other. He became the King of the Kingdom and lived with his queen happily ever after.